ly liked books.

much that whenever he finished
ate it. With a pinch of salt and a
at way, he could satisfy his appetite
well as his hunger. Which, by the way,

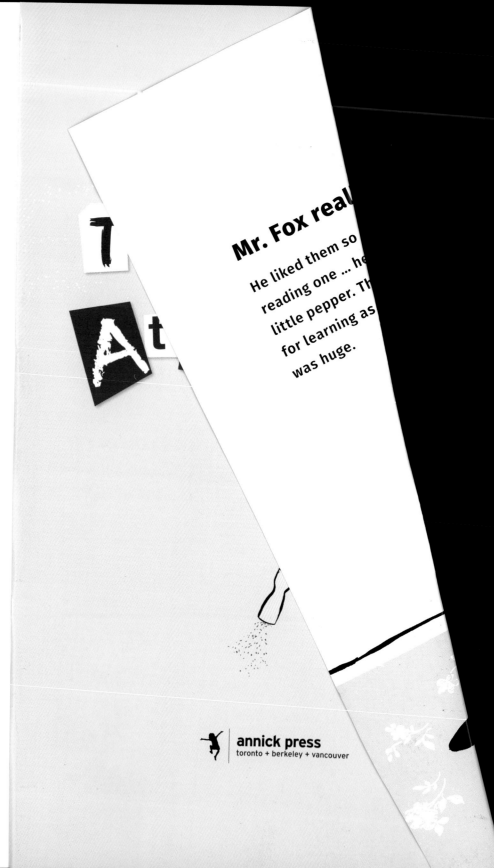

7

A

Mr. Fox real

He liked them so
reading one … he
little pepper. Th
for learning as
was huge.

annick press
toronto + berkeley + vancouver

Mr. Fox needed at least three square meals a day. But books were expensive, and after a while he couldn't afford them. So he sold most of his furniture and soon had nothing left but a table, a ratty mattress, and a rickety chair.

He spent all the money on new books, which filled his stomach and gave him **plenty of food for thought.**

The more books Mr. Fox consumed, the more his appetite grew. Soon his stomach was constantly grumbling.

But Mr. Fox was wily, and for some time he had been keeping his eye on a certain building. The building was full of books. It had more books than he'd ever seen— even more than his favorite shop, **THE CORNER BOOKSTORE**.

Whenever he went near this building, the heavenly scent wafting out of it made his nose quiver. It was the delicious *smell of paper.*

One day he walked into the building and found himself in paradise—row upon row of shelves filled from floor to ceiling with books!

Yum, yum, thought Mr. Fox.

But that wasn't all. You were allowed to take the books home, for free. He could hardly believe it!

After that, Mr. Fox went to the library every day. He casually surveyed the shelves, sniffing the air and smacking his chops. Sometimes he took a little lick of a page or two. When he found something to his taste, he tucked it into his tote bag and took it home.

Things went on this way for quite some time.

After a while, though, library patrons began to complain that pages had been nibbled, and that many books were soaking wet—and smelly! Other books had gone missing entirely. It was all very mysterious.

The librarian decided to investigate.

Mr. Fox came to mind immediately. No one else visited the library so often or looked the books over so carefully. And when the librarian really thought about it, she realized that he had never returned a single book.

From then on, she kept a close eye on his every move.

One morning, the librarian watched in horror as Mr. Fox ...

Sniffed at a couple of atlases before putting them back on the shelf in disgust ...

Then **moseyed** over to the Russian Classics section ...

Where he selected an especially **fine volume** ...

Then pulled out a **salt shaker** and **pepper grinder** ...

And, whistling contentedly, **generously seasoned** the book ...

Before taking a big **BITE!**

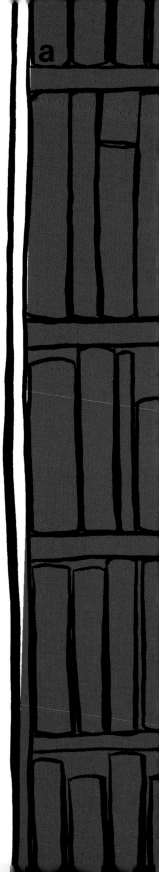

In no time, Mr. Fox had gobbled up the entire book for his breakfast, complete with dust jacket and bookmark.

The librarian jumped out of her hiding place. **"YOU BOOK CHOMPER!"** she shouted indignantly. **"Get your snout out of our novels this instant!"**

Mr. Fox struggled to swallow the last few pages. When he had finished every morsel, he looked up at the librarian with an innocent smile.

She was unmoved. "That is an inappropriate use of reading material," she said curtly. "From now on, Mr. Fox, you are forbidden from entering the library."

STO

Mr. Fox trudged home, totally
dejected. Hard times lay ahead.

Now that he'd lost his daily supply of books, he was forced to consume other reading material. Furniture catalogs, fast-food flyers, and free daily papers kept him fed for a while. In desperation, he even rummaged through the recycling bins behind his house.

But it was hard to stay healthy on such a poor diet. His fur soon lost its silky sheen. And the cheap paper upset his stomach.

At night he dreamt of fat 600-page novels. But when he woke up in the morning, his stomach was growling and there was not a book in sight.

Mr. Fox was desperate. So even though he was usually a law-abiding citizen (apart from the whole library business, that is)—

he cooked up a devious plan.

Mr. Fox dug out his Aunt Frieda's **ski mask**,
grabbed his tote bag, and headed straight for ...
The Corner Bookstore.

"Reach for the sky!" he bellowed. "This is a holdup!

Fill my bag with books right now!

If there's any funny business, I'll bite you in the bottom!"

That sounded quite frightening, so the store clerks quickly filled Mr. Fox's bag. He got away with

24 MOUTH-WATERING VOLUMES.

The bag was heavy!
Mr. Fox had to drag it home.

The moment he got inside, Mr. Fox began browsing through the books. He was **greedily wolfing down** his seventh course when the doorbell rang.

It turned out that Mr. Fox wasn't really cut out to be a professional thief.

"You're under arrest,"

a police officer shouted, "you sneaky, under-handed book thief, you!"

It seems that someone had recognized Mr. Fox, even with the ski mask. What rotten luck!

Mr. Fox tried to explain. He apologized a hundred thousand times. But it was no use.

"A crime is a crime," the officer grunted as he handcuffed Mr. Fox and hauled him off to jail.

And there Mr. Fox stayed, living on a diet of bread and water … and with absolutely nothing to read. **He had been denied all reading material** as part of his punishment.

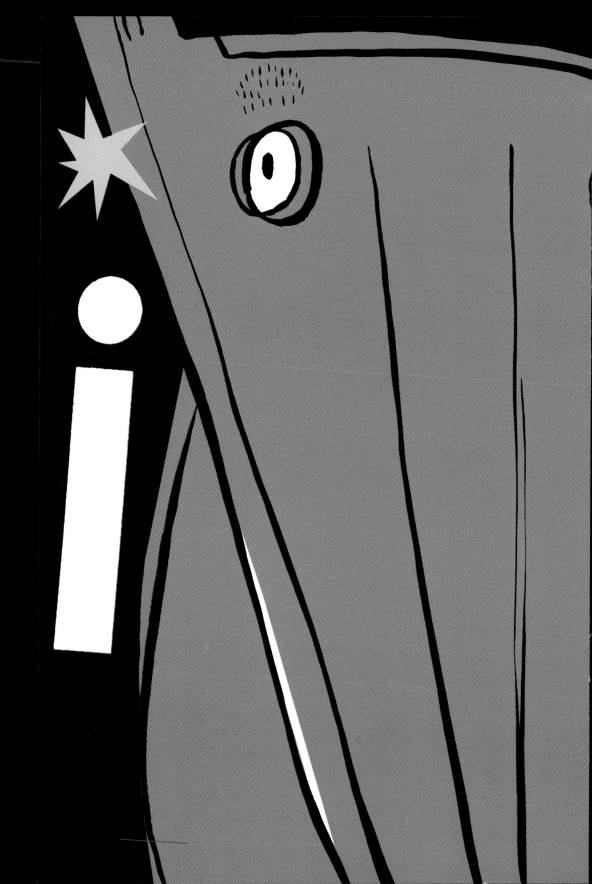

Mr. Fox didn't know how long he could last under such cruel conditions. Things were looking grim.

But one day, he had **an idea!**

Mr. Fox fawned over the guard, showering Mr. Schultz with compliments. **The flattery worked,** and Mr. Fox convinced the guard to bring him paper and pencils.

Now Mr. Fox scribbled day and night. Ideas practically poured out of his pencil.

Soon there were pages **everywhere.**

After about two weeks, the book was finished. It was a tasty 923 pages long—**about the size of a nice fat ham!** Mr. Fox was already drooling.

Mr. Schultz, who also loved to read, was delighted that Mr. Fox's novel was finally finished. The few lines he had glimpsed while delivering the prisoner's morning cup of tea had made him eager to read the whole story.

Because the guard had been such a big help and had been especially diligent about keeping the pencils nice and sharp, Mr. Fox allowed him to be the first to read his novel. He handed his story over to Mr. Schultz ... as a temporary loan, of course.

The story was **so exciting** that Mr. Schultz didn't go to work for two whole days because he couldn't stop reading. When he reached the end, he knew one thing for sure: Mr. Fox was one brilliant writer.

In fact, Mr. Schultz loved the book so much that he had nearly eaten a few pages himself!

So on his way back to work, he took a detour.

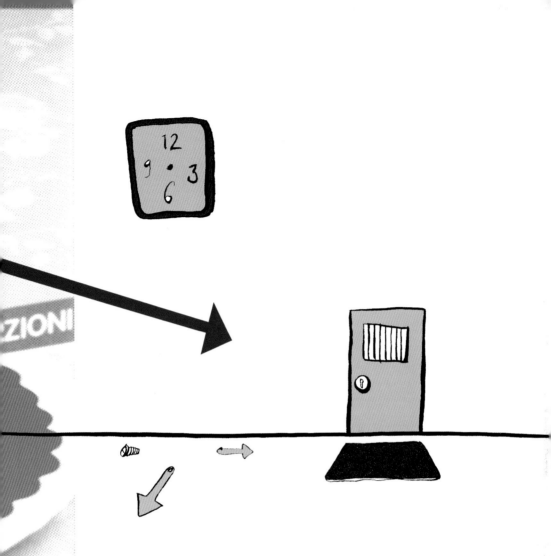

Meanwhile, Mr. Fox was getting more and more impatient. He couldn't wait to **fill his belly** with his book.

And when Mr. Schultz appeared at his cell door carrying the stack of pages, Mr. Fox jumped for joy.

Mr. Schultz went on and on about the book. Such cunning language! Such canny characters! Such a sly and surprising conclusion!

While the guard talked, Mr. Fox

ate

and listened

and ate

and

ate!

"Mr. Fox," said the guard when he had finished raving, "what would you say about making a real book out of your novel—one that people could buy in a bookstore?"

When he heard the word "bookstore," Mr. Fox flinched, and a few pages dropped out of his mouth. His last visit to a bookstore had landed him in jail! But he calmed down when Mr. Schultz explained that he wanted to publish the book.

"Okeydoke," said Mr. Fox, wiping his lips. "That's fine with me."

Luckily, the prison guard had a good reason for making his earlier detour—he had photocopied the entire book!

A good thing, since the original had just been devoured.

Prison Press

Prison Press

Press

Prison Press

The rest of the story unfolded like a fairy tale.

Mr. Schultz quit his job as a prison guard and started a publishing company. Mr. Fox's novel was a runaway bestseller, and was translated into 17 languages.

It was also made into a movie
that became a smash hit.

Due to his fame, Mr. Fox didn't have to serve the rest of his sentence. He was quietly released from prison, and his criminal record was swept under the carpet.

Mr. Fox was now a
FILTHY RICH MILLIONAIRE
and could afford to buy all the books he wanted. But his own books tasted the best. He became one of the most famous authors in the world. Many journalists interviewed him, and scholars studied his work.

But there is one question that still puzzles everyone.

Why does every novel by Mr. Fox come with little packets of salt and pepper?

© Franziska Biermann, represented by Susanne Koppe Agency:
www.auserlesen-ausgezeichnet.de
German edition © 2015 mixtvision Verlag, München
Original title: Herr Fuchs Mag Bücher!
English translation © 2016 Shelley Tanaka
English version edited by Debbie Rogosin

Annick Press Ltd.

Cataloging in Publication
Biermann, Franziska, 1970-
[Herr Fuchs mag Bücher. English]
    The fox who ate books / Franziska Biermann ; [translated by Shelley Tanaka].

Translation of: Herr Fuchs mag Bücher.
Issued in print and electronic formats.
ISBN 978-1-55451-845-6 (paperback).—ISBN 978-1-55451-846-3 (hardback).—
ISBN 978-1-55451-847-0 (html).—ISBN 978-1-55451-848-7 (pdf)

    1. Foxes—Juvenile fiction. I. Tanaka, Shelley, translator II. Title.
III. Title: Herr Fuchs mag Bücher. English

PZ7.B474F69 2016   j833'.92   C2016-900561-5
                                            C2016-900562-3

Distributed in Canada by University of Toronto Press.
Distributed in the U.S.A. by Publishers Group West.

Printed in China.

Visit us at: www.annickpress.com

Also available in e-book format.
Please visit www.annickpress.com/ebooks.html for more details.
Or scan